Teach Me...™
Everyday
FRENCH
Volume 2
Celebrating the Seasons

Written by Judy Mahoney
Illustrated by Patrick Girouard

Our mission at Teach Me... to enrich children through language learning.

The *Teach Me Everyday* series of books introduces common words, phrases and concepts to the beginning language learner through delightful songs and story. These engaging books are designed with an audio CD, encouraging children to read, listen and speak. *Teach Me Everyday Volume 2* celebrates the seasons and activities throughout the year. Follow Marie and her family as they venture out to the zoo, go on a picnic, visit museums, build a snowman and celebrate the holidays. The text is presented in a dual language learning format, meaning the French and English are side by side in order to enhance understanding and increase retention. The audio is narrated in French and introduces music memory through familiar songs. Children of all ages will enjoy exploring new languages as they sing and learn with *Teach Me*.

French is spoken in many countries around the world, not just in France. It is one of the Romance languages like Spanish and Italian. It is also the official language of the United Nations and the International Olympic Committee.

Teach Me Everyday French – Volume 2: Celebrating the Seasons
ISBN 13: 978-1-59972-201-6 (library binding)
Library of Congress Control Number: 2008902654

Copyright © 2009 by Teach Me Tapes Inc.
6016 Blue Circle Drive, Minnetonka, MN 55343 USA
www.teachmeinc.com

With respect to the differences in language, the translations provided are not literal.

Book design by Design Lab, Northfield, Minnesota.
Compact discs are replicated in the United States of America in Maple Grove, Minnesota.

Printed in the United States of America in North Mankato, Minnesota.
092009
08212009

10 9 8 7 6 5 4 3 2

INDEX & SONG LIST

LE PRINTEMPS
SPRING

L'ETE
SUMMER

L'AUTOMNE
AUTUMN

L'HIVER
WINTER

Tu chanteras, je chanterai
Tu chanteras, je chanterai
Nous chanterons ensemble
Tu chanteras, je chanterai
S'il fait beau ou mauvais.

You'll Sing a Song
You'll sing a song and I'll sing a song
And we'll sing a song together
You'll sing a song and I'll sing a song
In warm or wintry weather.

Words and music by Ella Jenkins.
Copyright © 1966. Ell-Bern Publishing Co.
Used by permission.

Je plante des graines pour cultiver des légumes dans mon jardin. Cette année je cultiverai des tomates, des poivrons et des carottes.

I plant seeds to grow vegetables in my garden. This year I will grow tomatoes, peppers and carrots.

mon jardin
my garden

Avoine, pois et persil poussent

Avoine, pois et persil poussent
Avoine, pois et persil poussent
Le sais-tu, le savez-vous
Si avoine, pois et persil poussent?

Le fermier plante les graines
Il respire, lève la tête
Tape des pieds, frappe des mains
Fait un tour admire son jardin.

Oats and Beans and Barley Grow
Oats and beans and barley grow
Oats and beans and barley grow
Do you or I or anyone know
How oats and beans and barley grow?

First the farmer plants the seeds
Stands up tall, takes his ease
Stamps his feet, claps his hands
And turns around to view his land.

Savez-vous planter les choux

Savez-vous planter les choux
A la mode, à la mode
Savez-vous planter les choux
A la mode de chez nous.

On les plante avec le pied...
On les plante avec les mains...
On les plante avec le nez...

les carottes
carrots

Do You Know How to Plant Cabbage
Do you know how to plant cabbage
The way we do it at home
Do you know how to plant cabbage
The way we do it at home.

We plant them with our foot...
We plant them with our hands...
We plant them with our nose...

la girafe
giraffe

le singe
monkey

l'âne
donkey

le lion
lion

Allons au zoo

Maman nous emmène au zoo demain
Zoo demain, zoo demain
Maman nous emmène au zoo demain
Pour tout le matin.

Nous allons au zoo...o...o
Pourquoi pas toi...toi....toi?
Viens avec moi...moi...moi
Nous allons au zoo...o...o.

Regarde tous les singes sauter dans les branches...
Regarde dans l'eau nager les crocodiles...

Going to the Zoo
Momma's taking us to the zoo tomorrow
Zoo tomorrow, zoo tomorrow
Momma's taking us to the zoo tomorrow
We can stay all day.

We're going to the zoo, zoo, zoo
How about you, you, you?
You can come too, too, too
We're going to the zoo, zoo, zoo.

Look at all the monkeys swinging in the trees...
Look at all the crocodiles swimming in the water...

Words and music by Tom Paxton.
Copyright © 1961, 1989.
Cherry Lane Music Publishing Company, Inc. (ASCAP).
All rights reserved. Used by permission.

neuf

le bateau
boat

le ballon
ball

Rame, rame, rame
Rame, rame, rame donc
Vogue le canot
Joliment, joliment
Joliment, joliment
Attaquons les flots.

Nageons, nageons
Nageons, nageons dans la grande piscine
Quand il fait froid, quand il fait chaud
Des plongeons dans l'eau
Yeux fermés et sautez, dans la grande piscine
Oh qu'il fait bon s'amuser toute la journée!

A la claire Fontaine
A la claire Fontaine
M'en allant promener
J'ai trouvé l'eau si belle
Que je m'y suis baignée
Il y a longtemps que je t'aime
Jamais je ne t'oublierai.

Row, Row, Row
Row, row, row your boat
Gently down the stream
Merrily, merrily
Merrily, merrily
Life is but a dream.

Nageons, nageons
Sing to the tune of Sailing, Sailing.

A la claire Fontaine
Traditional French song.

Soleil se lève
Soleil, vois le soleil
Soleil se lève je voudrais être chez moi
Soleil, vois le soleil
Soleil se lève je voudrais être chez moi.

Bosse la nuit jusqu'au matin
Soleil se lève je voudrais être chez moi
Charge les bananes jusqu'au matin
Soleil se lève je voudrais être chez moi.

Viens monsieur patron compter mes bananes...
Voilà six, voilà sept, voilà huit régimes...
Un beau régime de belles bananes...
Voilà six, voilà sept, voilà huit régimes...

Day-O
Day-O, me say Day-O
Daylight come and me wan' go home
Day-O, me say Day-O
Daylight come and me wan' go home.

Work all night 'til the mornin' come
Daylight come and me wan' go home
Stack banana 'til the mornin' come
Daylight come and me wan' go home.

Come mister tallyman, tally me banana...
Lift six hand, seven hand, eight hand bunch...
A beautiful bunch of ripe banana...
Lift six hand, seven hand, eight hand bunch...

Words and music by Irving Burgie and William Attaway.
Copyright © 1955, 1983.
Lord Burgess Music Publishing/
Cherry Lane Music Publishing Company, Inc. (ASCAP).
All rights reserved. Used by permission.

les peintures
paintings

Plus tard nous traversons la rue pour aller voir le musée d'art.

Next we go across the street to visit the art museum.

Regarde les peintures de Van Gogh. Les tournesols dans ses peintures ressemblent à ceux de mon jardin.

Look at the painting by Van Gogh. The sunflowers in his painting look like the ones in my garden.

J'aime regarder les taureaux dans les peintures de Goya. Je fais semblant d'être le matador.

I like to look at the bulls in Goya's paintings. I pretend I am the matador.

Tingaleo
Tingaleo, viens petit âne viens
Tingaleo, viens petit âne viens
Mon âne vite, mon âne lent
Mon âne viens at mon âne va t'en
Mon âne vite, mon âne lent
Mon âne viens et mon âne va t'en.

Tingalayo
Tingalayo, come little donkey come
Tingalayo, come little donkey come
Me donkey fast, me donkey slow
Me donkey come and me donkey go
Me donkey fast, me donkey slow
Me donkey come and me donkey go.

Tingalayo, come little donkey come
Tingalayo, come little donkey come
Me donkey hee, me donkey haw
Me donkey sleep in a bed of straw
Me donkey dance, me donkey sing
Me donkey wearing a diamond ring.

le chat
cat

la feuille
leaf

le râteau
rake

Colchiques
Traditional French song.

le maïs
corn

Avant de retourner à l'école, nous allons à la ferme de notre grand-papa. Nous donnons à manger aux vaches, aux poulets et aux cochons.

Before we go back to school, we visit Grandpa's farm. We feed the cows, chickens and pigs.

Mon grand-papa tond les agneaux. Plus tard, il nous promène dans un char avec nos cousins.

Grandpa shears the wool from the sheep. Later, he takes us on a hayride with our cousins.

A la ferme de grand-père

Ah, allons tout de suite, allons tout de suite
A la ferme de grand-père
Allons tout de suite, allons tout de suite
A la ferme de grand-père.

A la ferme de grand-père il y a une vache brune (bis)
La vache elle fait un son comme ça: Meuh! (bis)

A la ferme de grand-père il y a petit poulet rouge (bis)
Le poulet il fait un son comme ça: Cot! Cot! (bis)

Down on Grandpa's Farm
Oh, we're on our way, we're on our way
On our way to Grandpa's farm
We're on our way, we're on our way
On our way to Grandpa's farm.

Down on Grandpa's farm there is a big brown cow (repeat)
The cow, she makes a sound like this: Moo! (repeat)

Down on Grandpa's farm there is a little red hen (repeat)
The hen, she makes a sound like this: Cluck! Cluck! (repeat)

l'agneau
lamb

Baa Baa Black Sheep
Baa baa black sheep, have you any wool?
Yes sir, yes sir, three bags full
One for my master and one for my dame
One for the little boy who lives down the lane
Baa baa black sheep, have you any wool?
Yes sir, yes sir, three bags full.

Agneau blanc
Agneau blanc as-tu un peu de laine?
Oui monsieur, oui monsieur, trois sacs pleins
Un pour mon maître, l'autre pour madame
Un pour le garçon qui vit un peu plus loin
Agneau blanc as-tu un peu de laine?
Oui monsieur, oui monsieur, trois sacs pleins.

les poules
chickens

la vache
cow

Père MacDonald
Père MacDonald a une ferme, E – I – E – I – O
Dans sa ferme il y a une vache, E – I – E – I – O
Avec meuh ici et meuh là-bas
Ici meuh, là-bas meuh, partout des meuh, meuh
Père MacDonald a une ferme, E – I – E – I – O.

Dans sa ferme il y a une poule, E – I – E – I – O
Avec cluc ici et cluc là-bas...

Dans sa ferme il y a un chat, E – I – E – I – O
Avec meow ici et meow là-bas...

Dans sa ferme il y a un mouton, E – I – E – I – O
Avec baa ici et baa là-bas...

Old MacDonald
Old MacDonald had a farm, E - I - E - I - O
And on his farm he had a cow, E - I - E - I - O
With a moo, moo here and a moo, moo there
Here a moo, there a moo, everywhere a moo, moo
Old MacDonald had a farm, E - I - E - I - O.

And on his farm he had a chicken, E - I - E - I - O
With a cluck, cluck here and a cluck, cluck there...

And on his farm he had a cat, E - I - E - I - O
With a meow, meow here and a meow, meow there...

And on his farm he had some sheep, E - I - E - I - O
With a baa, baa here and a baa, baa there...

C'est Halloween.
Je sculpte un visage
dans mon potiron.

It is Halloween.
I am carving a face
on my pumpkin.

le potiron
pumpkin

Cinq petits potirons

Cinq petits potirons assis dans le noir.
Le premier a dit, "Mon Dieu, il est tard."
Le second a dit, "Sorcières dans le vent."
Le troisième a dit, "Ce n'est pas important."
Le quatrième a dit, "Partons maintenant."
Le cinquième a dit, "Non, c'est amusant."
"Hou-hou" dit le vent, la lumière s'éteint
Et les potirons roulent dans le jardin.

Five Little Pumpkins
Five little pumpkins sitting on a gate.
The first one said, "Oh my, it's getting late."
The second one said, "There are witches in the air."
The third one said, "But we don't care."
The fourth one said, "Let's run and run and run."
The fifth one said, "I'm ready for some fun."
"Oo-oo" went the wind, and out went the light
And the five little pumpkins rolled out of sight.

la lune
moon

le hibou
owl

Ce soir je porterai un costume de "Chaperon Rouge" et Médor sera le loup. Pierre sera un "cowboy". Après, nous irons "trick-or-treating" avec nos amis.

Tonight I will dress up in my Little Red Riding Hood costume and Médor will be the wolf. Peter will be a cowboy. Then we will go trick-or-treating with our friends.

Mois de décembre Month of December

la neige
snow

**Regarde, la neige tombe.
Allons jouer dans la neige.
Nous tirons nos luges, allons sur
la colline et glissons.**

Look, snow is falling.
Let's go and play in the snow.
We take our sleds
and slide down the hill.

**Plus tard nous faisons
un bonhomme de neige. Il a des
yeux de charbon, un nez de carotte et
un chapeau melon. Il porte l'écharpe
de ma mère.**

Then we will build
a snowman. He has
coal eyes, a carrot nose
and a derby hat. He wears
my mother's scarf.

Le bonhomme de neige

C'est un de mes amis
Le connais-tu aussi
Il porte chapeau melon
Est froid comme un glaçon.

Deux yeux de charbon
Un nez de carotte jaune
Deux bras faits de bâton
Et un manteau de neige.

Devines-tu son nom?
Ecoute les informations
Tu ne le verras jamais
Printemps, été, automne
Qui est-ce?

le bonhomme de neige
snowman

Snowman Song
There's a friend of mine
You might know him too
Wears a derby hat
He's real cool.

He has coal black eyes
An orangy carrot nose
Two funny stick-like arms
And a snowy overcoat.

Have you guessed his name
Or do you need a clue?
You'll never see his face
In autumn, summer, spring
Guess who?

Vive le vent

Vive le vent, vive le vent
Vive le vent d'hiver!
Qui s'en va sifflant, soufflant
Dans les grands sapins verts
Vive le temps, vive le temps
Vive le temps d'hiver
Boules de niege et jour de l'an
Et bonne année grand-mère.

Sur le long chemin
Tout blanc de neige blanche
Un vieux monsieur s'avance
Sa canne dans la main
Et tout là-haut le vent
Qui siffle dans les branches
Lui souffle la romance
Qu'il chantait petit enfant.

Jingle Bells

Jingle bells, jingle bells
Jingle all the way!
Oh what fun it is to ride
In a one-horse open sleigh, hey!

Sainte nuit

Douce nuit, sainte nuit
Tout est calme, et sans bruits
L'enfant dort dans les bras de Marie
Et sa mère, le regarde sourire
Amour aux cheveux dorés
Jésus, nous est donné.

Silent Night

Silent night, holy night
All is calm, all is bright
'Round yon Virgin, Mother and Child
Holy infant, so tender and mild
Sleep in heavenly peace
Sleep in heavenly peace.

Ce sont les fêtes.
Nous célébrons la fête de Noël.
Nous faisons des petits gâteaux
et décorons la maison.

It is holiday time.
We celebrate Christmas.
We bake cookies and
decorate our house.

les biscuits
cookies

le ballon
balloon

Si tu vas au ciel

Si tu vas au ciel, bien avant moi
Fais un petit trou que je passe par là
Si tu y vas, bien avant moi
Fais un petit trou que je passe par là.

Quand il y a, du beau soleil
Quand il y a du beau soleil
Dans l'univers, tu m'emmèneras
Fais un petit trou que je passe par là.
Voilà!

When the Saints Go Marching In

Oh when the saints, go marching in
Oh when the saints go marching in
Oh I want to be in that number
When the saints go marching in.

Oh when the sun, comes out and shines
Oh when the sun comes out and shines
I want to be in that number
When the sun comes out and shines.
Yeah!

Maintentant nous connaissons les mois de l'année. Et toi? Au revoir!

Now we know the months of the year. Do you? Goodbye!

janvier	January
février	February
mars	March
avril	April
mai	May
juin	June
juillet	July
août	August
septembre	September
octobre	October
novembre	November
décembre	December

Teach Me...
VOCABULAIRE
Vocabulary

LE PRINTEMPS
SPRING

bonjour	hello
le jardin	garden
les légumes	vegetables
les fleurs	flowers
le lion	lion
la girafe	giraffe
le singe	monkey
l'anniversaire	birthday
la fête	party
le gâteau	cake
le jeu	game

L'ETE
SUMMER

la plage	beach
le seau	shovel
la pelle	pail
le maillot de bain	bathing suit
le sable	sand
les nuages	clouds
le bateau	boat
le fromage	cheese
la banane	banana
le pain	bread
les fourmis	ants

L'AUTOMNE
AUTUMN

les châtaignes	chestnuts
le chat	cat
le chien	dog
l'arbre	tree
le râteau	rake
la ferme	farm
les agneaux	sheep
la vache	cow
les potirons	pumpkins
le loup	wolf

L'HIVER
WINTER

la luge	sled
le bonhomme de neige	snowman
la carotte	carrot
l'écharpe	scarf
la nuit	night
Bonne Année	Happy New Year
les bonbons	candy
le masque	mask
mes amis	my friends
au revoir	goodbye